To Lin
With Best w[ishes]
Love from
        June, 2000

CW00996393

POETIC JUSTICE

Elaine Watwood

MINERVA PRESS
LONDON
MIAMI DELHI SYDNEY

POETIC JUSTICE
Copyright © Elaine Watwood 2000

ISBN 0 75411 023 0

First Published 2000 by
MINERVA PRESS
315–317 Regent Street
London W1R 7YB

Printed in Great Britain for Minerva Press

POETIC JUSTICE

For my Mum, and in loving memory of my Dad

The New Recruit

I really am now a man in blue,
Achieved my ambition, this is true.
Uniform pressed, boots of a shine,
Know I must not step out of line.
In theory everything seemed so great –
I did not know about the hate.
Wearing the uniform makes me proud –
I didn't know drunks were so loud.
Love the demanding day-to-day life –
Didn't know the worry it would cause my wife.
Love the excitement of the night shift –
Must never let my concentration drift.
Love walking around my beat –
Some people I don't want to meet.
All the fresh air is good, I say,
Better than an office and more pay.
No one told me about the rain,
Or complainants wanting to know my name.
Love working on the motorway –
Didn't realise idiots would be out today.
Love to be working in the sun,
But the fog and snow are no fun.
Love crossing the children over the street;
Drivers are impatient and love to bleat.
Love teaching the kids not to get drugged,
Hate dealing with grannies getting mugged.
Love to help clear up the crime rate,
Giving evidence, expecting some bait.
Love working as a member of a team,
Love my days off, rare as they seem.
However, is this really a job I need?

With all the advice I have to heed,
The police force is a way of life.
I talk it over with the wife.
Never a dull moment, or so she's heard,
Variety has to be the keyword.
She knows, as I, our feelings are such
I would never enjoy another job so much!

Life

'Life,' the judge said as he sat in court.
For this, the barrister had really fought.
When you talk about 'life' there are many meanings,
Certain aspects cause a variety of feelings.
No one has said that life is fair;
We all know it causes some despair.
Life can be funny, life can be sad,
Life can be good, but sometimes bad.
An old friend used to say quite a bit:
It's not a dress rehearsal, this is it!
This is life, to be lived to the full;
You should never waste time being dull.
Life can be short, life can be long,
It doesn't depend on whether you do right or wrong.
The only thing that anyone can ever suggest
Is whatever life deals you, do your best.

Initiation

'At the end of my tether, with being his wife,
So I've killed him', she said, 'with a kitchen knife.'
Over the phone she had her say
One dark, desperate, horrible day.

Just my luck! My colleague had gone,
Left on my own, no help, none!
I joined the police force to have a life,
But didn't expect this sort of strife.

The woman went on and told me the harm.
My heart beat quicker, I had sweat on my palm,
My hair started to stand up on end,
Must remember my training, needed a friend…

'What shall I do?' she pleaded with me.
'Do nothing else,' I said rather shakily.
Then to my horror and real disgust,
I heard her laughing – in me, no trust?

Then I realised it was my colleague Di
Wanting to initiate me – it was a good try.
On the phone I now listen very hard –
It's made me be always on my guard!

Love is Blind

Our eyes met across the crowded room.
I hope he comes over so very soon!
He looked at me, his eyes were warm,
A night with him I wouldn't want the dawn.
I fluttered my eyelids to let him know
That I hoped his interest would grow and grow.
I smiled at him, he didn't smile back;
Perhaps I was losing my cultured knack.
Shuffled around to get his attention;
He looked so great, a real sensation.
His eyes were twinkling straight at me –
How I hoped he was single and very free!
Making love with my eyes, he was too,
It was a lovely feeling, something new.
Then the host of the party spoke to me,
Asked me to dance if I was free,
But I wanted to know about the man so fine.
'Oh, him in the corner,' he said, 'he's blind!'

Victims

'They come into our homes to take our goods.'
The victims' tears can come in floods.
'They don't give a damn; they poison our homes.'
No one listens to the victims' moans.
'It isn't a matter of the property we've lost,
It's the intrusion into lives at some cost.
The house feels dirty and no longer mine...'
This will be so, for a very long time.
If the burglar knew the effect it had,
Would he reconsider being such a cad?
It's the goods they're after and nothing more;
Do they know how it hits right to the core
When they're selling off our property in the pub?
Think of the victims, I wish they would,
Not of the property that we have all lost,
But the effect on our lives at some cost.
All you can do now is hope and pray
That they get burgled too one miserable day.
Only then will they completely understand
Why committing burglary just has to be banned.

The Ageing Rock Star

His devoted fans are all around
Waiting to hear his booming sound.
Then he's here, he's on the stage;
He doesn't really look his age.

His leg kicks high without a moan,
He thrusts his hips and makes a groan;
The audience all go really wild
As if they all were only a child.

He sings his old songs to the joy of the crowd;
The concert hall shakes, it is so loud.
Young and old enjoy him the same,
Over the years he's become good at his game.

Everyone knows every single line;
All are having such a great time.
Two hours on, the end is nigh;
It's not unusual to have a little cry.

The Flasher

'There's a flasher in the bushes!'
The old sergeant gushes.
Get out with your dogs,
Of course, in plain togs.
There will be help around
If this man can be found.
Into the park the young policewoman was sent.
To catch him, she had every intent.
Not long after he suddenly appeared;
At the policewoman he invitingly leered
Naked as the day he was born.
The dogs just didn't like all this porn –
At him they suddenly leapt.
His clothes on, he wished he'd kept.
They sunk their teeth into where it mattered,
And the flasher felt just extremely battered.
He limped off howling to hide away.
The policemen around really made his day!

People Watching

Going out to lunch on a certain day...
People watching – a game I like to play.
In the local pub all are there,
I have to try just not to stare.

There's the gambler on the one-armed bandit,
Continually giving it just one more chit,
The man on the pool table cueing to the right
And a lad at the bar having a quick bite.

The dartboard is full of arrows thrown;
Players' accuracy has grown and grown.
Dominoes are knocking on the table;
To win, they all think they are able.

The drinkers are all achieving their goal,
All out of work, and drinking their dole.
The big screen is showing a football match,
A woman in on the lookout for a good catch.

Some furtiveness going on in the corner,
The other side of the pub feels so much warmer.
Senior citizens are having a budget meal
Where they know it is a very good deal.

Youngsters are there listening to music,
All very bold, feeling safe in their clique.
The barmaid has a nice, welcoming smile,
An interesting place, for a while.

Domestic Dispute

I'm nineteen and sent to this house
Where man and wife had begun to grouse.
They were old enough to be my mum and dad
But I was expected to sort out the problem they had.
You side with one, and then the other,
My inexperience I was trying to cover.
The more they argue, the more it means
There will be no compromise, or so it seems.
How do I now get out of this?
Future disputes I hope I miss.
My uniform states I know it all
But it feels like I'm hitting against a brick wall.
Then the argument appears to turn,
The man's face becomes rather stern.
He sounds like he is blaming me –
To the problem, have we found the key?
It's my fault, so they can get on;
Back on patrol, job is done!

Fat

Some say I look like skin and bones.
The doctor, my mum usually phones.
In the mirror I just see fat,
Enough extra meat to feed the cat.
Now I am down to a size eight,
Old clothes in my wardrobe I so hate.
Mum says I have got to get bigger,
But I love my new little figure.
The doctor says I'm making myself ill;
Lose more weight I think I will.
Some boy told me I looked too thin,
But I feel great, I went and told him.
Although I don't always feel so well,
Eating food makes you fat, I can tell;
When I've eaten I look in the mirror
And I can see all the fat on my figure.
No one believes me that I do feel fat –
I'm overweight and that is that.
Now I believe as I get older
Feelings for me may get colder.
They say it's an illness, all in the mind,
But I'm getting fatter, and a cure they must find.

A Sight For Sore Eyes

On a very cold winter's night
A cardboard box is their plight.
They always seem to own a dog,
In the wheel of fortune just a cog.
Good Samaritans hand out soup
To this troubled, underprivileged group,
By day, beggars upon the street
Just trying to earn their keep.
It is a sight for sore eyes,
But can sometimes be a surprise.
Are all of the beggars homeless too?
It's hard to tell, this is true.
Some beggars rarely want any food
And, when rejected, can get rude.
Do we give them a copper or two,
Or something even better in lieu?
Some beggars just get up and go home,
Leaving the homeless to justifiably moan.

Fun in a Bun

The lad and his wife started to play.
'Feel like a bite to eat?' he heard her say.
He thought, Right, we'll have some fun,
And put his marriage tackle inside a bun.

'Here, come and have a bite of this,'
He said, hoping it would be nothing but bliss.
Of course, he forgot about his dog
Who suddenly became all agog.

Never seen anything like this before –
It must be a new toy, he felt sure.
Quick as a flash, Monty took a bite,
Much to the amusement of the wife.

The poor lad didn't know what to do –
His intimate parts were looking blue!
Later, as he surveyed his stitches,
He regarded it as one of life's hitches.

But what was he to tell the lads?
And just think of all those gags!
'Never mind,' his wife said with glee.
'I wasn't really very hungry!'

Motherhood

Today should be a real treat,
Lots of nice things adoringly to eat,
Savoury bits and sweet items too,
All made lovingly, by a mum so true.

The child opens his presents with some glee,
Mum's memories go back, remembering painfully
All that effort, midwife shouting loud,
The look of her husband, so very proud.

All the sleepless nights, no time for rest,
When tired, regarding him as a little pest,
All the illnesses each child has to go through,
Nursed by Mum when he's feeling so blue.

All the anxiety of starting at school,
Although a wrench, Mum remains so cool.
The joy of realising he's achieved his dream
When he tells you he's got onto the football team.

The trials and tribulations of each exam he takes,
The uncertainty of each new friendship he makes,
Then it's leaving school, university for a time,
More exams, girlfriends, hope everything's fine.

Then it's concern that he gets a good job,
When everything works out, time for a sob.
Mum's thoughts suddenly come back to today –
Married man with children now, memories far away.

Who Forgot Jesus?

Nativity time, little children gathered around,
Teacher making adjustments to Angel Gabriel's crown.
The Three Wise Men look so sincere and cute,
The Kings, with their gifts, forget their route.

Joseph and Mary are practising with the crib,
Pick up Baby Jesus by the strings of his bib.
The next time they take him out of his bed
They promptly just drop him, right on his head.

It's the big night, the audience is there,
The Innkeeper is speechless and starts to stare.
The angels are having trouble with their wings.
Everything will be all right, but where are the Kings?

Then everyone stares into the crib –
Where is Jesus? He's not there, just his bib.
'I have forgotten to bring him,' a little girl states.
'Never mind,' says teacher, as a bundle she makes.

What if someone sees there is no one there?
Children upset, teacher in despair.
'We'll just leave him sleeping in his cot,
We won't tell anyone that Jesus we forgot!'

The Miser

He's now so old and set in his way,
But he just never wants to pay.
The heating he will not turn on,
Maybe I should be long since gone.

I sit here freezing in my home,
Even too cold to use my comb,
But he expects me to wait on him.
Of course I do, I must be dim.

I married him a long time ago –
The signs were there, I should know.
Then, he never put his hand in his pocket –
I remember he gave me some second-hand locket.

Often now I just sit and stare,
Sometimes feeling real despair.
My family asks why I didn't leave –
I hoped things would improve, I had to believe.

You can't explain your devotion to your man.
With warts and all, accept him, I can.
Now I'm so old and set in my way,
I know I'll love him to my dying day.

The Hairdresser

The hairdresser willingly spreads the rumour
About Mrs Smith's son and Mr Jones's tumour.
They snip away and carry on their chatter
About the woman down the road who's getting fatter.

All I want is that my hair is cut well,
But it is snipped away as enjoyable stories they tell.
You look in the mirror with some alarm,
Not wanting your hair to come to any harm.

Scissors in hand, a powerful tool they make;
Now we're hearing about a new dish to bake.
They carry on snipping, now causing concern,
Coming here, am I ever going to learn!

All I want is that my hair is cut well,
But it is still snipped away as the stories they tell.
Next time I may have a new hairdresser to call,
If I've any hair left on my head at all.

Sunday Dad

Times have really been so bad,
Now I find I'm just a Sunday Dad.
A couple of hours in the park we play,
If it's cold and wet they don't want to stay.

'But where do we go from here?' I say.
Where can you take two young children to play?
We sit in the burger bar for a little time
Sit talking, trying to make everything fine.

Now it's off to the local zoo again,
Same old animals, they're glad we came.
'But where do we go from here?' I say.
Where else can we visit, and, for a time, stay?

The children are getting fed up, I feel.
Seeing their dad like this doesn't seem real.
I know I must now take them back to Mum;
It's heartache. Is this really much fun?

St… Stuttering Patience

Take a statement, it must be true.
You have to listen, as you haven't a clue.
Hear the words the woman uttered,
But no one told me that she st… stuttered.

Each question I asked with due concern,
But, oh, am I ever going to learn?
It took some time for her to answer the questions;
She didn't want to listen to my suggestions.

It's very difficult to keep your face straight
When asking questions about certain times and date.
Although there is sympathy, it can be quite funny –
You want to laugh until there's an ache in your tummy.

After an hour and a half listening to the st… story,
I just hope she doesn't appear before a jury.
Back at the station, Sergeant said with a frown,
'Why didn't you let her just write it down!'

Snow

The snow glistens and lies around
Out at night, not hearing a sound.
Strange marks embedded in the snow,
Not knowing what's been around, friend or foe.

It's so white and crisp and lies deep in places.
People try to remove it, causing red faces.
All piled up it remains for days,
If you leave it alone it just fades.

The trees and shrubs lined with the snow
Bend with the weight and hang so low.
Bird tables and baths have a white trim,
The pond seems full right to the brim.

It's white all over, pretty, but a pest,
To many drivers it can be a good test.
It's now the birds are not around to sing –
Never mind, it's soon going to be spring.

The Office Party

It's that time of the year
When people are full of good cheer.
They have arrived and look so proud,
The music and chatter is very loud.
The lurex clings to every bump,
Women do not wish to look a frump.
Tight, short skirts so revealing,
Are they really so appealing?
Bleached, blonde hair looking lank,
Some look a mess, to be quite frank.
Mutton all dressed up as lamb –
But they really don't give a damn.
They're here to enjoy the party,
Don't mind for once looking tarty.
It will soon be time again to look their best,
But it's nice from the office to have a rest.
Heads spin and they start feeling woozy,
Didn't realise the boss was quite so boozy!
People appear in a different light,
Affairs starting, well, they just might.
It is hoped that in the cold light of day
There are no regrets – it was all just play.

Baby Blues

Oh, what will be my fate?
I'm late, I'm late, I'm late…
I think I'm having a do,
This feeling is so new.
Will it be a boy or a girl,
Or is my body just having a whirl?
Maybe it's just a laugh,
Or shall I get a baby bath?
I'm in a quandary – what shall I do?
I cannot stand all that baby poo!
I've looked to see, there must be a star,
I really do not want to be a ma.
Shall I get a baby pram,
And indeed a cuddly lamb?
Oh, what will be my fate?
I'm late, I'm late, I'm late…

Naughty Boy

I know I am not a naughty boy,
I am really just a little coy.
Oh, I know I can be so very dense
When I climb over your new fence.

I know into my basket I drag your mat,
If we had one, I would blame the cat.
I know your slippers I often chew,
My tellings-off – there are quite a few.

Your garden I like often to wreck,
And then I think, Oh what the heck.
I know I have an irritating bark,
But really I'm having quite a lark.

I know I am not a naughty boy,
I am really just a little coy.
My name is Sam, and I want to play a game
Catching the ball, then I know I'm not lame.

I know we like to go to bed –
I lie so close, sometimes on your head.
When you yawn, making all that noise,
I sometimes respond as I cuddle my toys.

I know now I must be calm,
I don't want to go to that farm.
Your attention I seek, your patience I try,
It's because I love you, Mum, that's why.

My Best Friend

My best friend is only ten inches high.
He's certainly been a very good buy.
I had him years ago when I was two,
Now I'm eighteen our love is true.
I tell him all about my hopes and fears,
He comforts me when there are tears.
I take him with me wherever I go,
Sometimes where it doesn't show.
The fact that he is there makes me strong.
My teddy and I have a real, true bond.
He was wrapped in paper one Christmas Day –
As soon as I saw him, I had my own way.
Since then he's been to bed every night –
He's there if my dreams cause a fright.
Although I have lots of cuddly bears,
There are none like Ted; my thoughts he shares.
Now I look at his once fine hair –
He really is now rather threadbare.
I cuddle him gently if we are sad,
I need him to last, this real fine lad.
I want him to see me through the years to come
So I can tell him about future plans and the fun.
I want us to share everything with glee,
My best friend, Ted, and me.

Seasons of Fun

It's wintertime – the snow lies deep,
The children sledging finish in a heap.
They squeal with delight as they enjoy their play;
Travelling adults wish it would just go away.
They are clearing their cars and defrosting the same;
Slippery roads, traffic jams – it's all such a pain.

It's springtime – the gardens are full of new flowers
But it can be windy too with plenty of showers.
The empty trees are bursting into life,
Little lambs gambol with no strife,
Daffodils are swaying in the breeze –
Nice to know we no longer freeze.

It's summertime – the sun shines brightly,
Watering the plants at least once nightly.
Off to the sea to have a paddle,
On the beach we like to dabble.
Too much sun finishes with you in bed
Unless you wear a hat on your head.

It's autumn time – leaves begin to fall,
Birds get twitchy, to each other they call.
The weather cools, sweaters on, we say,
Need to work in the garden each day.
Turn the central heating on till it's full –
Wintertime is coming; it's going to be dull.

Night Patrol

On a misty, dark, troubled night,
Whilst walking the beat you may feel fright.
Where it is really dark, places you don't know,
They have to be checked out for any foe.
You depend on your torch to give some light
On a misty, dark, troubled night.
When the wind blows, a sound from up high,
You see the culprits when you look to the sky.
The magnificent flagpoles swaying in the breeze –
I hope my break comes quickly, before I freeze.
Down dark alleyways, shadows on the wall,
Is there someone there? Will they answer my call?
Checking the doors, hope they are all locked,
Guarding premises that are all well stocked.
In a rear dark alley, strange feeling in tummy,
Then I realise it is only a tailor's dummy.
The deafening silence is hard to break –
A cat jumps out, now I'm really awake.
You carry on, the mist is getting thicker,
I can't help but think of Jack the Ripper.
Suddenly my radio crackles into life,
Controller asking if I have any strife.
So reassuring to hear a friendly voice;
Must continue on patrol, have little choice.
Look forward to my break in warm, cosy light,
On this misty, dark, troubled night.

Retirement

Now I sit at home and stare,
From my relaxing armchair,
I think of those days that are now past –
Oh, am I getting old too fast?
I think of working as a member of a team,
Every incident forms part of my dream.
All the laughter and the joy,
You wonder if it was all a ploy.
I remember working at such a pace,
Everything to be done with indecent haste.
Now I sit at home and stare,
From my relaxing armchair,
I think of when it's a frosty morn,
All I do is turn over and yawn.
I now have time for friends, old and new,
When shopping, I now have time to queue.
I'm in my garden tending the flowers,
Enjoying the sun, and even the showers,
I go for days out, walks and entertain too;
Retirement is great – I just hadn't a clue.

What Diet?

'I feel hungry and my tummy rumbles;
I'm on this diet again,' she grumbles.
Why does everything I like to eat
Just increase the size of my seat?
They tell me to eat vegetables and fish,
But I prefer a good pastry dish.
I'm supposed to eat healthy salad teas,
But I'd rather have fish, chips and peas.
After my dinner I can't have a sweet
If I want to look all slim and neat.
Weigh food out is what they suggest,
Or you may increase the size of your chest.
I buy larger clothes to disguise the fact
That with the slimming club, it is a broken pact.
I'm supposed to eat food with reduced fat,
But I'm off to the fridge instead to have a good snack.
And when again I step on the scales,
My poor face just visibly pales.
'I feel hungry and my tummy rumbles,
I'm on this diet again,' she grumbles.

Drunkenness

The lad comes crashing through the door:
I look at him – he is a sight to abhor.
His eyes are glazed, his speech of a slur,
He bawls, 'Get my solicitor, I want to speak to her.'

Then he vomits and starts shouting loud
As if he is playing to a large crowd.
The Sergeant orders, 'Get him to a cell.'
After a night's sleep he should feel well.

The lad's response is to begin to fight,
Foul language uttered with all his might.
The dawn breaks, the cell is quiet,
It appears he no longer wishes to riot.

He reappears very respectful and so calm.
Is it the same person who wished such harm?
Very well spoken and a nice lad too,
What a pity his other side we had to view!

Show him the video, can't believe it was him,
Makes excuses, had to blame the gin.
Hope next time he controls the booze
Or, yet again, his liberty he will lose.

Freddie Kruger

The film I saw was *Nightmare On Elm Street*.
After it, I did not wish to eat.
Freddie Kruger was a frightening sight
On that dark, creepy, lonesome night.
Then I went to bed with my dear wife
And something started to give me strife:
I could hear scratching on the wall.
Was is a beast about to maul?
What was it, I wanted to know:
Was it a friend or some foe?
My wife said, 'I know about this –
It's Freddie Kruger, that's who it is.'
Quick as a flash I leapt out of bed –
Freddie Kruger had gone to my head.
Then I sat in the kitchen all the night
Underneath the glow of my comforting light.
Next time I think I'll borrow a Luger
So I can shoot that Freddie Kruger.

Motorway Madness

It's pouring with rain,
This is such a pain.
I'm driving my car
Not so very far
But it's on the motorway.
Idiots are out to play,
The wet and all the mist…
Do you get the gist?
Why do they go so fast,
Don't they want to last?
People do love speed;
Advice they will not heed,
Lanes they love to hog
Even in all the fog.
When will they learn?
Only when they burn?

My Fear

I really do not like all this water –
I am, after all, my mother's daughter.
Mum just never learnt how to swim
After someone went and pushed her in.

Her fear has now come out in me
Although, no excuse, it happens, you see.
At school swimming lessons once a week
I found myself to be just very meek.

Chlorine in the pool smelt so bad,
After dipping a toe, enough I'd had.
Wouldn't take my feet off the floor –
If I did, I felt so insecure.

Didn't like getting my face so wet –
Everything would just make me fret.
Always had a feeling I was going under,
My face was often black as thunder.

So I played hockey and netball instead
Then I slept much better in my bed.
Now, every time I think of swimming,
It just sends my head spinning.

Is There Anyone There?

I feel so sad,
Can it be that bad?
Fear there is no hope,
I just cannot cope.
Life is full of despair;
Is there anyone there?
I have tried so hard,
Always on my guard,
On my own it seems,
Anyone hear my screams?
They just do not care;
Is there anyone there?
The doctor gives me pills,
But it's all these bills,
My children to feed,
Feel I've gone to seed,
Family doesn't seem aware.
Is there anyone there?
Then I see some light,
Someone hearing my plight,
A person you cannot see –
I feel so free.
My problems he and I share;
There *is* someone there!

Jealousy

I can feel so jealous; I do not know why,
Suspicious, although I realise he does try.
I have been let down before and suffered a lot;
Therefore, I must appreciate just what I've got.
Room for improvement, must change my way,
Because I really *do* want him to stay.
Everything between us has been so good,
Why can't I be happy, like I know I should?
A life of torment, it seems to be –
Does he prefer someone else to me?
How can I have peace of mind?
My obsession is a real bind!
I just want him to be true to me,
How can I be certain he's not free?
My jealousy, I must let it drift away
Because I want to be with him every day.

Infatuation

I always drag myself out of bed
And go to the place I really dread.
In the classrooms, the cross-country run,
It rarely is very much fun.

However, I sometimes sit and often drool,
Nothing to do with subjects at school.
My teacher has such a lovely smile –
Oh, to be in his company for a while!

My imagination can be very vivid;
He asks me a question, I'm really livid.
I did not hear what he said to me
Because I was elsewhere, you see.

Embarrassed, my face begins to burn,
Didn't want him to see me having a turn.
Daydreaming, he just had to scold;
Now I just think he is rather old!

So I turn to boys of my own age –
Their feelings, too, difficult to gauge,
More interested in football and smoking.
Find a boyfriend? You must be joking!

Why can't they be mature and nice to know
So all my love can blossom and grow?
Hope they learn so very soon –
Over them, I would like to swoon.

Now, I must start thinking things over –
Perhaps I will be better off with my dog, Rover.
He is mature, loving and always there,
Our feelings for each other, nothing to compare!

Racing Certainty

I often go to the track –
The horses I love to back.
Place my bets on a real nag
Until no money left in my bag.
Why do I think I'm going to win?
Always go out on a limb!
I seem to have really caught the bug.
Stop it – I don't think I could!
Bookmakers are the real winners,
People like me are the sinners.
Instead of giving money to my wife,
Prefer the track, more exciting life.
One day I'll have a real big win –
It will then cause such a din.
Will I then give the money to her?
No, instead more debts I will incur.
I wish I'd taken to drink instead,
Then I'd just crash out on my bed.
Now I think the time must be right
To get some help with my plight.
I must pray to him up above
Because I will need his special love.

Cats

T S Eliot wrote a very good tale;
Of course, this was not about to fail
As Lloyd-Webber made it into a show.
To see it, I really just had to go
Enjoyed the fantasy of make-believe cats,
But in reality they just drive me bats.
There are four of them next door to me,
I don't want more. Why? You'll see.
Into my garden they often roam;
I just want them to slink off home.
They love to come and dig a big hole;
To leave a deposit, they think it's their role.
When the car is out on your drive,
Paw prints on it, cats are lucky to be alive.
These felines need some urgent attention,
But nothing to cause a real sensation.
Birds they chase, they ruin the new plant;
At them, I often just have to rant.
Very curious, and quick as a flash
Before my teeth really start to gnash,
The she-cat stares, I feel the vibes,
She says, 'Remember, we each have nine lives!'

Winter Blues

Check that the heating is turned to its full;
Wintertime is coming and you may feel dull.
Motorists clearing their cars and defrosting same,
Slippery roads, traffic jams – it's all such a pain.
When sitting at home cold and in a huddle,
Wishing someone would just give you a cuddle,
Think of spring and all the new flowers,
Beautiful greenery enhanced by showers,
Empty trees bursting into new life,
Little lambs gambolling with no strife,
Daffodils swaying in the breeze,
Someone will always give you a squeeze.
Think of your blessings, how many there are,
Family, friends, your children – the best by far.
When you are really feeling so blue,
Think of the love, people have for you.
Immerse yourself in your family's good tales;
Winter will go quickly, this never fails.
No longer will you have the heating on high;
The blues will be gone, I do not lie.

Divorce

All the anger, all the pain –
I'm not ever getting married again.
I can't believe our love was so true,
Now it's hate – you can't compare the two.

It's hard to accept that we got so low –
We argued over a lampshade, he had to go.
I cannot understand why we parted,
Our marriage had only just started.

The line between love and hate is so thin –
I realise now, also too late for him.
We should have worked harder at staying together
But, in fact, we were both at the end of our tether.

Dividing our home was no great joy –
What about the dog? He was a good boy.
You think it's just between him and me,
But the pain also hits the family.

I hope now I can have peace of mind
And that people will just be very kind.
Our friends, I hope they don't go away –
I need to rebuild for another day.

Rain (Summer 1998)

When is it ever going to stop?
Good for the garden, but only a drop.
It just continues to rain and rain,
Overflowing that ugly huge drain.
I look out of the window – what is there?
Puddles, flooded fields, cattle in despair.
I never thought I'd have a sea view –
When I bought my house, I hadn't a clue.
When is it ever going to stop?
Are all my plants going to rot?
This year I bought a new garden seat –
To sit on it would be a real treat.
It just continues to rain and rain;
Maybe, next year, it won't be the same!

When I Am Famous

I work very hard on a building site
But at weekends I fly my own kite.
Monday to Friday the going is tough;
After the weekend, on Mondays, I feel rough.
Scaffolding without gloves feels like ice –
The treatment of my hands is not very nice.
Back-breaking work just to earn my keep,
My thoughts sometimes run very deep.
When I am famous, will I remember all this?
I will then have a lovely life of bliss.
I hope I can keep my feet on the ground
With all the notoriety I will have found!
You must always remember your grass roots –
I'm thinking of this, as I pull on my boots.
Back to my work in fine weather and rain,
Digging holes, bricklaying with much disdain.
Why do some people have to work so hard?
My secret thoughts I have to guard.
Hopefully, I won't freeze for the rest of time –
Up the career ladder I hope to climb.
When I am famous I will treat others well –
They too will have their stories to tell.

Bonfire Night

The night is glowing just like the sun,
Everyone wrapped up warm, having some fun.
People standing in little huddles,
Probably preferring some warm cuddles.
The sky lights up, the children exclaim,
Why on November the fifth does it often rain?
The bonfire's glow makes us feel good,
People searching for even more wood.
Crackling, sparkling rainbows of showers,
Beautiful colours we see in our flowers.
Tasting chestnuts, hot dogs and the rum,
Fountains of sparkles, glad we could come.
Rockets roaring, the wheels are spinning,
The crowd now has just started thinning.
Time to go, bonfire is full of smoke,
Guy has gone, voices start to croak.
The air is damp and rather misty too,
Time for home, nothing left to view.

Heroes

They fought for us, so we are told,
Those courageous men who were so bold.
They were not given a chance, sent to war,
Many lives lost, had to be hard to the core.
You listen to the tales, try to imagine the scenes,
Try not to be put off when you hear the screams.
They were only boys, and not yet men;
We have great respect for all of them.
They had no choice, they had to go,
Frightened, and could not let it show.
In the trenches the fighting was grim;
Our lads had to say it was me or him.
They died for our country so we could be free.
We remember them, enjoying our lives of liberty.

My First Date

I'm fifteen. My name is Kate.
Today's the day of my first date.
How shall I look, what shall I wear?
And what am I going to do with my hair!

I'm in my bedroom, trying to contemplate,
I must be on time and not late.
Shall I hold his hand or give him a kiss,
Or just tell him stories about my big sis?

Where shall we go, what shall we do?
I hope I don't get in a real stew!
Shall I tell him this, or tell him that?
I hope he doesn't think I'm too fat.

Why are the butterflies busy in my tum?
I've known him for ages, it should be fun!
Shall I wear trousers or my new dress?
I hope he doesn't think I look a mess.

Oh, there's a knock at my front door.
Is it him, the boy I adore?
He looks at me with a huge smile –
It's going to be great, he's got style!

Boobs

Some are round and so fat,
Some are little and so flat.
Some are heavy and so low,
Reasons why I don't know.
Some are pointed and stick out,
Some are inverted and cause doubt,
Some are plastic, have a good shape,
Some are lively, keep you awake.
Some are spongy, feel like dough,
Reasons why I don't know.
Some are wayward, no control,
Follow you over when you roll.
Some are bouncy, hit you in the face,
Can get black eyes when at pace.
Some are droopy, no feel of ease,
Especially when they reach your knees.
Some are perfect, give you a glow,
Reasons why I don't know.

Insomnia

In my bed tossing and turning,
Mind games playing, everything churning.
Try again to count more sheep,
I really must get some sleep.
Look at the shapes on my wall,
Try to figure out them all.
Very hot, push my covers off,
Then I just begin to cough.
Start to think of the next day –
What to do, must have my say.
It's 2 a.m., the milkman calls,
Feel like climbing up the walls.
Try again to count more sheep,
I just cannot get off to sleep.
Start compiling my shopping list,
Think of opportunities I have missed.
Write that report in my head,
Get up and remake my bed.
Soon the birds tell me it's dawn,
All I want to do is stretch and yawn.
Next thing my clock is showing eight –
Oh no, now I'm going to be late.

Hockey

Onto the field marching we went,
Ready to win, not to relent.
Sticks are ready, heads bent down,
Positions are filled, ball's on the ground.
The whistle blows and off we go,
Take a push-in, game begins to flow.
Up the field quick as a flash,
Opponent tackles, down with a crash.
To score a goal you must get through,
Hurting wrists, feet and ankles too.
Lovely sound when you hit the backboard,
Excitement when realising you have scored.
Players must hit the ball so hard –
Watch yourself, be on your guard.
Hockey balls can cause real pain,
Then you won't be happy that you came.
Half-time, have a little rest,
Coach informs you you are the best.
Second half, try to score again –
This really is a good close game.
Opposition scores, we all feel down,
From the coach we get a frown.
We raise ourselves to try and get one more –
Little did we know what was in store.
Opposition given a penalty flick,
Score again just as quick.
The whistle blows, end of the game –
All our efforts were in vain.
Off the field skulking we went,
Did not win, had to relent.

The Christmas Fête

Brown Owl has to be their substitute mum
When all of the Brownies are having such fun.
They chatter to their friends and don't listen at all
When doing their gluing in the church hall.
It's Christmas time, decorations to make –
Go to the toilet before it's too late.
Glue in the hair instead of on paper –
It's really becoming a right old caper!
'Phillipa, don't do that,' Brown Owl moans.
'I will send you all back to your homes.
Jessica, are you really listening?'
Rather than the paper, Rosie's face is glistening.
The angels' legs are on back to front, but
All Brown Owl does is have a quiet grunt.
The snowmen have their heads on upside down
And just where is Angel Gabriel's crown?
The Christmas trees look rather battered,
As if it all really mattered
Because Brown Owl knows it's not too late
For everything to be ready for the Christmas Fête.

Protest

They're opening a new bypass near to us –
I expect there will be the usual fuss.
There are tree houses, tunnels, banners and flags,
People dressed scruffily, some in old rags.
So many of them, where are they from?
When security arrives, they appear to have gone.
The tree fellers creep onto the land,
All protesters making a stand.
The fierce battle is a sight to be seen –
From deep in the wood you hear a scream.
Loud hailers roar, the music plays loud,
Together they make an aggressive crowd.
No one wins, and all becomes calm,
Bailiffs and protesters come to no harm.
The environment must be protected at all cost,
But motorways are necessary – on some this is lost.
Everyone is entitled to their own views;
Confrontations always make the news.
What the answers are, no one knows,
But passion in people grows and grows.

My First Flight

I had to be persuaded, I didn't want to go,
But I was in need of the sun's glow.
Went to the airport, my stare transfixed –
The aeroplanes all looked like plastic.
My knees were shaking, I looked rather pale,
I think this trip is about to fail.
Where are my travel pills? Left them at home –
I really just do not want to go to Rome.
Try to eat, I feel so sick,
In my neck I'll get a crick.
My friends say, 'Have a drink,'
All I want to do is think.
The next thing I know I'm on the plane –
I'm not enjoying this game.
The engines roar and up we go,
My stomach churns, friends are foe.
Air hostess gives the drinks out free –
I have a few, oh what will be!
Gradually I feel so much better,
To my friends now I've become a debtor.
With the drink I get quite loud,
Really laugh at the passing cloud.
Eat my food with the utmost glee,
Enjoying myself I chat merrily.
Then we're down to earth with a bump
And in my throat comes a lump.
I've just thought, I've got to do this again,
Just to get back from where I came!

The Doctor's Surgery

Here we are all sitting around
In the waiting room, not making a sound.
An old woman starts talking to me –
She seems to want to know my history.
I hear all about her aches and pains
And then about the trouble with her drains.
The man in the corner starts to cough,
Lady at the back looks rather off.
Then a boy comes in with a pronounced limp and
A woman shouts, 'I need a drink.'
Another chap has an irritating twitch
And a young boy starts to itch.
Then the babies start to cry;
My throat just feels dry.
A girl arrives, she's got a big spot,
With a scruffy man who's had a drop.
Lady appears with her arm in a sling,
Then a little lad with a bee sting.
Compared to these, I feel fine –
I think I'll come back another time!

Prejudice

I can't help the colour of my skin –
It's the fault of my kith and kin.
I know my face is so very black,
But prejudice I feel I lack.

Why isn't everyone just the same?
There must be someone to blame.
Authority, I feel, always picks on me –
Is it because I'm from another country?

But I know I was born in Leeds,
Still, my protests no one heeds.
The colour of my skin gets in the way
As I go about my business from day to day.

If in trouble I expect the worst,
Being black can be a curse:
I seem always to get the blame,
On my family it just brings shame.

When there are so many fights
I always blame the whites.
It's their fault, nothing is new –
Could I be prejudiced too?

Redundancy

Go each fortnight and sign on the dole
For my family and me, a daunting role.
They can't understand what has happened to me,
Made redundant, they just let me go free.
I try to tell people how I'd like to work.
They stereotype, but I don't want to shirk.

Go to the job club each and every week,
A good working day is what I seek.
I just can't lie in bed any more,
Got to get up and complete some chore.
Now I've started some voluntary work –
On this, there is no time to shirk.

I work very hard to be at my best –
Redundancy, got to get it off my chest.
All I hope is that I be employed full-time –
Can't this voluntary job be permanently mine?
Doing it as a volunteer is all very good,
But pay me for it, I wish they could.

Christmas Shopping

Queuing for this, queuing for that,
Got to get a present even for the cat.
Tills are jingling, money is spent,
Bank balances are in for a huge dent.
Shops are decorated and look so bright –
Talking Christmas trees, what a fright!
There are toys, gifts and cards everywhere,
Will there be any money to spare?
Shopping gets heavy, a rest is due,
Have a mince pie and a drink too.
A jumper for Mum, shirt for Dad,
What about Aunt Elsie's young lad?
The crowd seems in such a rush,
They are now even starting to push.
Down the escalator, this can be trying,
Everyone determined to carry on buying.
Got the turkey and the Christmas pud,
The Christmas crackers, hope they're good.
It's now all over, have no fear,
Thank goodness it's only once a year!

Young and Old

As I wander down the street
How my knees do often creak.
Over the years, my hair was blonde;
Now it's grey, where's the magic wand?
My joints ache, I don't see so well,
Is this really a life of hell?
Before too long, I have a fear
That also I may not quite hear.
Sometimes, my memory just goes blank;
My hair, too, is thinning and lank.
However, I do really feel well –
Is it really a life of hell?
I look at life both present and past,
Hope I'm not getting old too fast.
You look at the young, so full of life,
Enjoying themselves with little strife.
Work hard, play hard is their game;
If this is so, there can be no shame.
You listen to all their anxious tales,
Offer advice, hope it never fails.
We all know, we have been there too,
Experience of life has seen us through.
All our memories the young wished they had;
Therefore, getting old can't be that bad.
As I wander down the street
Young and old I like to meet.

The Deal

When I was thirteen I had a bike.
I was so pleased, no longer did I have to hike!
But then I realised how dangerous it could be
To cycle on the roads where traffic flows free.
Cars rushed close by, didn't give me a chance,
If I landed on the road just hoped I'd bounce.
Then on very wet days the cars would splash,
Didn't give me a minute they were in such a dash.
An experienced car driver I have now become –
These dreaded cyclists are no real fun.
All over the road they sometimes are –
It's a very close thing as they brush my car.
I try to give them a real wide berth,
But some of them think they own the earth.
Consideration is required by both, I feel,
For safety's sake I hope they have a deal.

The Collector

The collector rattles his tin;
Shall I put some money in?
What is the collection for,
Is it for something I abhor?
Then I am told it is for AIDS,
My enthusiasm just fades.
I believe they are all to blame –
I'm afraid I have little shame.
Someone says, 'But I had a transfusion –
This must not lead to confusion.
It was no fault of mine.
I have not committed any crime.'
Time to start to think again:
These sort of people seek no fame.
How can I be so rash?
I start to search for some cash.
The collector rattles his tin,
I quickly put some money in.

Addiction

The colours are mixing on the wall,
Can't get up, think I might fall.
I take a look at my left arm,
All punctured with a sweaty palm.
How long is it since I had a fix?
Feel like I want some more kicks.
I must get out to meet my dealer
Instead of trying to see a healer.
My head thumps, I feel so bad,
This addiction, I wish I didn't have.
How did it start? If only I knew.
Problems, I have had a few.
Not everyone takes to a drug –
Shake it, I wish I could.
Now I'm off to a secret meeting,
Feeling as if I've had a good beating.
It won't be long before I feel great,
But afterwards is the time I hate.
To feed my habit, I've become a taker;
It won't be long before I meet my maker.

A Dedication

Work hard, play hard, out each day,
Very loyal, you want to earn your pay;
Get on with people, you should know you're liked,
Then all your dreams just get spiked.
The doctor had a lot to say...
Must learn to cope day by day
With support from the family and your friends.
Although this illness seldom ends,
You know you are going to get through
With all the love people have for you.
Always a smile upon your face
Despite this disguising heartache.
You must continue the way you've been,
Your determination held in high esteem.
Enjoy yourself so life feels warmer,
Remember, no one knows what's round the corner.

Blow Into This

Out at night having a drink,
No time really to think;
Have one for the road, people say,
No time for the next day.

On the way home police lights are flashing,
Know from the wife will get some earbashing.
'Blow into this,' the smart officer asks,
You just think of that beer in all those casks.

My heart is pounding, my pulse in a race,
Blowing into this causes a red face.
'Now let me see,' the officer says with concern.
'It's negative. Carry on, from this I hope you learn.'

I got in my car as quick as I could,
Never looked back, I felt so good.
Now I think of that night – what a hoot!
He never saw the stolen property in my boot!